Tucked into the sandy cliff top, in a bay shel
towering stacks, Peata Ruadh peeked out of
burrow. Peata Ruadh's tummy was rumbling! Inside
the cozy burrow the sound of his tummy rumbling
echoed as loud as thunder.

He didn't want to wake up
the other puffins with his
thundering rumbling
tummy. Today he was
going fishing.

"Listen to the noise my tummy is making" he whispered to his Papa, "I'm going to starve if I don't get any fish today." Peata grumbled. "I could eat a whale. Twice."

Papa stood back, his large orange feet padding up and down in the grass, looking at the size of Peata. He chuckled "I don't think you would feel very well if you did that, but I do wonder how many fish you could eat?"

Peata, being very hungry said "Lots and lots and LOTS."

"It's a tricky business fishing, you know" warned Papa. "You need a plan" he advised "it won't be long until you are the best fisher puffin." he said.

Peata took a little stroll through the grass, trying not to listen to his rumbling tummy.

"A *plan...*" thought hungry Peata... but he didn't seem to have a plan.

"*I really need a fishing plan*" Peata squawked.

In his burrow, he closed his eyes. He hoped a plan would come into his head.

In the middle of the afternoon, Peata waddled from his burrow, flew off the cliff top, round the stacks and out to sea.

He flew out over the rolling waves, until he came to another stack. There were clouds of puffins flying around the stack.

Peata perched on the edge of the stack and he slowly lowered his beak to touch the water. Peata gently pushed down into the water with his orange feet still firmly planted on the rock. He got himself ready to catch fish.

He opened his beak... and sang.

It was the most beautiful sound.

Slippery silvery scrumptious sandeels,

Swim to me for dinner deals,

Slippery silvery scrumptious sandeels,

Please be enough for delicious meals.

Peata didn't even catch the tiniest of sandeels. His tummy grumbled and rumbled. He watched as puffins disappeared completely through the water coming back up with beaks full of sandeels.

"What a disappointment! What a disaster! What am I going to do now?" thought Peata, hungrier than before.

Back in his burrow, Peata closed his eyes and tried to think of another fishing plan.

The next afternoon, he flew off the cliff top, round the stacks and out to sea. He flew over the gentle waves and back out to the fishing stack. He landed on the edge of the fishing stack.

He lowered his head below the water and opened his eyes.

It was very busy. Hustle and bustle. Sandeels and puffins everywhere he looked. He took a deep breath and hurled himself onto the water with a big splash.

He tumbled and spluttered, toppled and splashed.
Herding the sandeels like sheep to the surface
of the water. But not even one sandeel
for supper.

*"What a disappointment!
what a disaster!"
What am I going to do
now?"* thought Peata,
the hungriest he had
ever been.

Peata sat on the fishing stack with his head just below the surface of the water. He carefully watched. Peata watched puffin wings and puffin beaks.

Then Peata ruffled his feathers and stretched. He folded his wings tightly to his body and gracefully slipped under the water.

He joined the other puffins. With gentle flutters of his wings he flew through the sparkling, bubbling water, opening his beak as he steadily flew through the shoal of sandeels.

Peata stacked each sandeel he caught to the back of his beak. He stopped them from falling out with his strong raspy tongue.

He only headed for the surface of the water when he could not fit any more sandeels into his beak.

Papa puffin was waiting for Peata on the fishing stack.
"What a catch" Papa said, complimenting Peata.

"You must have at
least 10 fish in your
colourful beak.
You have a very
good fishing
plan now."

Papa reminded Peata that he sang for his sandeels. He would not let Peata forget how he herded the sandeels like sheep.

Together they spread their wings, and flew back over the sea, around the isles and skerries to the sandy cliff top where lots of puffins were watching Peata bring home his first dinner.